MW00942727

Series by Tevin Hansen:

Junkyard Adventures:

Word Dragon

Sea Serpent of Science

Giant of Geography

Alien of Astronomy

Mermaid of Music

Art Monster

Hairytale Adventures:

The Birthday Bear

The Museum Guide

The Zookeeper

Halloween Adventures:

The Halloween Grump

The Haunted Hospital

The Halloween Space Adventure

Handersen Publishing, LLC
Lincoln, Nebraska

A Junkyard Adventure #1
Word Dragon

This book is a work of fiction. All characters and other incidents are a product of the author's imagination. Any resemblance to actual events, or persons, living or dead, is entirely coincidental.

Text copyright © 2019 Tevin Hansen
Cover copyright © 2019 Handersen Publishing, LLC
Cover Art by Sarah Lowe
Interior Design by Nichole Hansen

Manufactured in the United States of America by West Wind Litho, West Valley City, Utah

All rights reserved, including the right of reproduction in whole or in part in any form.

Summary: A visit to Uncle Larry's junkyard turns into a magical adventure for Eli and Grace. They must play a dangerous game of Scrabble with the Word Dragon if they want to return home.

Library of Congress Control Number: 2018910941
Handersen Publishing, LLC, Lincoln, Nebraska

Paperback ISBN: 9781947854291
Hardback ISBN: 9781947854307
eBook ISBN: 9781947854314

Publisher Website: www.handersenpublishing.com
Publisher Email: editors@handersenpublishing.com
Author Website: www.tevinhansen.com

A JUNKYARD ADVENTURE

Tevin Hansen

Handersen Publishing, LLC
Lincoln, Nebraska

Meet Uncle Larry

The junk store on Broadway Street had a million things for sale. And the man who owned the shop had a million stories to tell.

His name was Uncle Larry.

The sign out front...

Uncle Larry's
Antique Shop

...wasn't a complete lie.

There really were antiques inside his store. There were old lamps, paintings with fancy wood frames, art sculptures, baseball and hockey cards, jewelry and furniture, old collectible toys, and lots of other things.

The junkyard was out back.

Uncle Larry had a bunch of junky old cars that didn't drive anymore. He had rusty cars, and smashed-up trucks that would cost so much to fix that it was cheaper to buy a new car.

Uncle Larry's store had some of the coolest stuff on the planet. Decades worth of junk and antiques were packed, racked, and stacked into his crowded old shop on Broadway Street. His apartment was just above the store.

Uncle Larry was a friendly old man who loved to sell things and talk to people. He never married, and never had any children, but he loved to tell stories to kids while their parents shopped in his store.

If it was okay with their moms or dads, or whoever they were out shopping with, Uncle Larry would grab his old brown leather stool, plunk right down in the middle of the store, and tell a story.

Uncle Larry had a million stories to tell.

And they always came true.

CHAPTER

1

Ice Cream

Eli and Grace thought Dad was kidding when he said they were going to a second-hand store. They were headed downtown in the family SUV.

"It's a hand store?" asked Eli, who had just turned nine years old. He'd never heard of such a thing. "A store that sells robot hands and fake hands and stuff like that?"

"No, Eli," said Dad. "A second-hand store means they sell items that are used. The original owner sold them or gave them away. I think you kids nowadays call it a thrift shop."

Eli curled his fingers into claws and tried to grab his younger sister.

"Stop it!" said Grace, who was seven years old. She smacked her older brother's hand away. "I don't like it when you scare me."

Dad continued down Broadway Street. It was fun to watch all the shops and cars go past.

"Today, we're going to see if Uncle Larry's has a good, used lawnmower," said Dad.

"LAWNMOWER?!" said Eli and Grace. They both groaned as Dad pulled into the parking lot with the big sign:

If you can't find it at Uncle Larry's... It doesn't exist!

"You told us we were going out for ice cream!" Eli complained. "That was the whole point of this trip, Dad. Remember?"

"We *will* go for ice cream," Dad told them, "just as soon as we're done here, at Uncle Larry's. Because the whole point of this trip is that we need a new lawnmower. Remember?"

Eli and Grace agreed that Dad was right.

Uncle Larry's opened at 10 a.m. And since it was just past ten o'clock, there were no other customers. Their car was the only one around.

"Okay, troops! We're here," said Dad. He spun around in the front seat to talk to them. "Now, when we go inside, you're allowed to look..."

"We know," said Eli. "Look but don't touch."

Dad nodded. "And please don't–"

"–break anything," Eli finished. "We know the rules, Dad. We're not kids anymore."

"Oh, right," said Dad. He winked at Grace, who gave him a goofy smile, which made him laugh.

As a family, they headed into the junk store.

And life would never be the same.

2
Harvard

Da-ding! Da-ding!

Bzzzzzzzzz-zuzz-zuzz....

The antique bell above the door rang, then it kind of fizzled out. It was for sale. There was a $12.00 price tag on it.

Everything at Uncle Larry's was for sale.

Everything except the guard dog, Harvard.

Harvard the Golden Retriever was snoozing in his favorite spot. An old rug that was covered in dog hair, which also had a price tag on it–$4.00.

"Hi, boy! How's Harvard today?" Dad reached down to scratch him behind the ears. The big scruffy dog loved every second of it.

Harvard gave a big, loud, happy bark.

"Harvard! Be quiet, please!" said a voice from the back of the store. "I'm trying to tally up yesterday's sales totals...what few there were. Tuesday will be a better day, just you wait and see. Wait—today is Tuesday, isn't it?"

Dad smiled at Eli and Grace. Then he stood up and hollered, "It's Wednesday, Larry!"

"Oh! Hello!" said Uncle Larry, as he hurried from the back to greet his first customers of the day. "Come in, come in! Welcome to the finest antique store on Broadway–"

CRASH!

Something made of glass hit the floor and broke into a million pieces.

"Oh, you old klutz!" Uncle Larry scolded himself. "You're supposed to *sell* things, not break them!"

Then he knocked over something else.

"Yee-ouch!" cried Uncle Larry, when he stubbed his toe. He was trying to be quiet and *not* embarrass himself, but it wasn't working.

"You okay, Larry?" Dad asked him.

"Oh, fine," said Uncle Larry. "You'd think after all these years, I'd know my way around my own store..."

Eli and Grace giggled. Dad held up a finger to his lips, but he was also trying not to laugh.

Then Uncle Larry appeared.

CHAPTER
3
Uncle Larry

Uncle Larry's smile was missing a tooth on one side, but it was a great big happy smile. He loved having customers in his store, and he also loved talking to people.

Dad had started shopping at Uncle Larry's Antique Shop & Junkyard a few months ago. He came in looking for a cuckoo clock for Mom, as a funny gift for her birthday. Mom's birthdays were always for fun, and to remember her by.

Even though Mom passed away two years ago, they continued to celebrate her birthday. Dad tried a bunch of online stores, but those clocks cost hundreds or even thousands of dollars.

At Uncle Larry's shop, Dad found the perfect, slightly used cuckoo clock for $22.00.

"Good morning," Dad said to Uncle Larry. "Sorry about, um...whatever broke. I hope it wasn't too expensive."

"Umm..." Uncle Larry stared at their dad, trying to sort through his memory for a name.

Uncle Larry was terrific at remembering kids' names, but he always had a hard time remembering the names of grownups–the ones who actually spent money in his store.

"Don't tell me, don't tell me..." Uncle Larry scratched his stubbly chin, trying very hard to come up with their dad's first name.

"Bill?" said Uncle Larry.

Dad shook his head.

"Brian?"

Again, Dad shook his head.

"I know it starts with a B," said Uncle Larry. "So it must be...Bob?"

"No," said Dad.

"Bart?"

"No."

"Bumbledore?"

"You mean, Dumbledore," said Dad, laughing. "From the Harry Potter books."

"No, that's not it..." Uncle Larry was having fun trying to guess their dad's name. He tried three more times, each of them incorrect.

"Ben," their dad told him. "Ben Fernandez. Or Benny, I suppose. Or Benjamin."

Eli and Grace used to always giggle when their mom called their dad by his first name, Benjamin.

Uncle Larry smacked his leg, saying how close he was to guessing the correct name. Then his greenish-yellow eyes sparkled when he looked down at the kids. And since Uncle Larry was kind of short, he didn't have to look down too far.

"And you must be Eli," said Uncle Larry.

Eli looked surprised because he'd never met this man before. "You...you know me?"

Uncle Larry laughed. A great big laugh that could rattle the junk that filled all the shelves.

"Well, not exactly," said Uncle Larry, "but your

father told me all about you when he was in here...
last month?"

Dad agreed. "Well, it was more like two months
ago. You helped me find that cuckoo clock."

"Oh, that's right," said Uncle Larry. "Now I
remember."

Uncle Larry dropped down to one knee,
somewhat painfully, so that he could meet Grace
while acting like a knight–a scraggly knight with
knees that popped, but still a knight.

"And you, my dear, must be Grace," said Uncle
Larry, then he bowed his head, which showed
that he didn't have much hair left on top.

"I hear that you are a wonderful dancer," Uncle
Larry said to her. "Your dad told me all about it
when he was in my shop. We talked about how
well you dance, and how hard you practice."

Grace smiled. "I'm in dance class! I'm working
on my please...um, plee-yays..."

"Oh, plié!" said Uncle Larry. "Yes, yes. I'm sure
you don't want to see *me* try one of those. I'd
probably fall over. But I do have some old VHS

tapes that could help you learn some of those tricky ballet moves. Though, I suppose nobody uses those clunky old VHS tapes anymore, do they? And I probably have some old ballet shoes around here...somewhere."

Grace crossed her arms and said, "Ballet shoes are called slippers."

Uncle Larry was impressed. "I stand corrected, young lady. You are right. I meant to say ballet *slippers*, not shoes. Silly me."

Dad and Eli laughed because they knew Grace didn't mess around when it came to dance.

"Well now!" Uncle Larry clapped his hands, then rubbed them together. "What are we shopping for today? Door hinge? Shovel? How about a mini-fridge? Just got a couple of those in last week..."

"Well, actually, we need–" Dad stopped, then looked at Eli and Grace. "That is, I am looking for a lawnmower. These two are only interested in ice cream after we're done shopping."

"Then you came to the right place," said Uncle

Larry. "I have several lawnmowers to choose from..." Then he and Dad stepped aside to talk business.

Eli and Grace played with the dog while the grownups talked about boring lawnmowers.

"Hi, Harvard," said Eli, scratching behind the dog's ears, the same way he saw his dad do it.

Harvard tried to lick Eli's face, but he managed to keep the drooling doggie tongue away.

Grace just let him slobber away.

"Gross!" said Eli. "He just drooled all over you!"

"Dogs drool," said Grace. "So do you. I've seen your pillowcase with the drool spots."

Eli disagreed. "I do not drool in my sleep."

"You do," Grace said. "I don't ever lie."

"Yeah, right," said Eli, shaking his head.

"It's not your fault, Eli," she said. "Even your name is a lie. But instead of spelling it L-I-E, you spell it E-L-I."

Uncle Larry came back about two minutes later. Their dad wasn't with him.

"While your father is out back searching

through my collection of used lawnmowers," said Uncle Larry, "he agreed that I could tell you a quick story while we wait."

"A story?" said Eli.

"Sure, why not?" said Uncle Larry. "Despite what you may have heard, it's all the wonderful stories that make the world go around, not all that other stuff."

Eli wanted to explore the junk shop, not sit and listen to a boring old story. Then again, Dad did say they weren't supposed to touch anything. And where's the fun in exploring such a cool old shop if you're not allowed to touch anything?

"Your dad won't be more than a few minutes," said Uncle Larry, "so we'll have to hurry."

"Yeah, story time!" said Grace.

Uncle Larry reached behind one of the many tables piled with antiques and junk. He pulled out an old brown leather stool to sit on. The stool had a $6.00 price sticker, marked down from $9.00.

Eli and Grace sat down in front of Uncle Larry, right on the slightly used area rug, priced at

$14.00 OBO, which stood for "or best offer."

Harvard the dog was in between them. The scruffy old dog wanted to hear the story too.

Stories are not always safe.

Eli and Grace were about to find out just how dangerous stories could be.

4
Junk

"Are you both ready?" asked Uncle Larry.

"Ready!" said Grace. She was excited.

Eli only nodded, though he was curious about what kind of story Uncle Larry would tell.

Adventure story?

Survival story?

Scary ghost story?

"Okay then, here we go!" said Uncle Larry, then he got up from his stool and walked off.

Eli and Grace sat on the floor, looking around, wondering what happened to their story. Their storyteller just up and walked away.

"Now, let's see..." Uncle Larry's voice came from

somewhere around the corner. He was digging through all sorts of junk. He shoved things out of his way, searching the shelves for...something.

"Feather duster? No," said Uncle Larry. "Old broomstick? Nah, no good. Not for this adventure, anyway..."

While they waited, Harvard the dog tried to lick Eli's face again. This time, he let him, but only a little. Not the full doggie drool treatment.

"Here we go, this is perfect!" cheered Uncle Larry. "Ooh, and this! And that! This, too!"

When Uncle Larry came back, he was carrying several junk items in his arms.

Hubcap.

Rope.

Board game.

"These items, right here, are all important for your story," said Uncle Larry, then he handed out the junk shop treasures.

Eli was given the old hubcap.

Grace was given the rope.

Uncle Larry went back and forth between the

two of them, then he finally handed Grace the board game with the ripped up box.

Scrabble, a word game.

The used Scrabble game had a $2.00 price tag on it. There was also a yellow sticky note stuck to the top of the box.

1 letter 'N' missing

"What's all this?" asked Eli.

"That's your story!" said Uncle Larry. "What you are holding in your hands are magic items. You'll need them to complete your adventure."

Eli and Grace were both confused. They didn't understand how an old hubcap, a length of rope, and a Scrabble game (missing one letter 'N') was supposed to equal a story.

Uncle Larry pointed to the back door. It was the same door they'd seen their dad walk through just a few minutes ago.

The junkyard.

"Follow me!" said Uncle Larry, then he headed for the back of the store. He waved his hand, urging them to come along.

Eli and Grace followed him. So did Harvard, who also liked to go on adventures...unless it was nap time, or lunch time, or dinner time, or scratch-behind-the-ears time.

"This way!" said Uncle Larry, leading them through the store. He went around shelves, and tables, and piles of junk, and heaps and mounds of trinkets and knick-knacks, and glass display cases, and stacks and racks of more junk.

Among the stacks of junk and the piles of stuff, there was an old wooden door. There was a sign above the door.

JUNKYARD ADVENTURES

Eli and Grace were about to find out that the stories Uncle Larry told were magical stories.

And they always came true.

"This will be your first story," explained Uncle Larry. "There may be others, if you wish. But you must first survive this adventure."

"Survive?" Eli looked nervous.

"What's out there?" asked Grace.

"Is it the junkyard?" wondered Eli.

"Is Daddy out there?" asked Grace.

Uncle Larry held up his hands to stop them from asking too many questions.

"For your father, it's a lawnmower," explained Uncle Larry. "That's what he is seeking. For you two, it's something else. Adventure? Danger? A daring escape? Or maybe all three!"

Eli decided a long time ago that he was well past the age of make-believe. But Uncle Larry seemed to truly believe every word he told them.

"What do we do?" asked Eli. "Just..." He waved his hand toward the door.

"That's right, Eli," said Uncle Larry. "Simply step through that door." He stepped aside so Eli and Grace could go into the junkyard.

Neither Eli or Grace moved a muscle.

"If you're too nervous to see what awaits you, don't feel bad," said Uncle Larry. "We can just wait here until your father is done looking for his lawnmower. Or you can both help me clean up the shop a bit? I have a broom over there, and some cleaning supplies..."

Eli said, "No, thanks. We'll check it out."

Uncle Larry looked pleased.

Eli put his hand on the door knob, then turned it. He opened the door just a bit, barely enough to peek outside.

"WAIT!" Uncle Larry waved his hands in the air, trying to stop Eli before he could open the door all the way.

Then it would be too late.

5
Through the Door

"Did I ever tell you kids the story about the Word Dragon?" asked Uncle Larry.

Eli and Grace stood frozen to the spot. They both looked worried at the mention of a dragon.

"There's a dragon out there?" asked Grace.

"Cool. I know all about them," said Eli. "I've read a ton of books about dragons."

"Not like this one, Eli," said Uncle Larry, and shook his head. He looked so serious.

"What kind of dragon, then?" asked Eli.

"The dragon you're about to meet is a Word Dragon," said Uncle Larry. "And he's probably the smartest creature you could ever know."

"What's a Word Dragon?" Grace whispered to her brother.

Eli had no idea. But he was pretty sure they were about to find out.

"If you choose to take on this adventure," said Uncle Larry, "you have to complete it, otherwise you shouldn't even start. Once you begin...you must finish."

Eli was starting to doubt the whole thing. But he was still curious enough to at least check it out. He guessed that as soon as the door opened, they would find Dad looking at used lawnmowers.

Uncle Larry searched his pockets. His face lit up when he found what he was looking for.

"Oh! I almost forgot," said Uncle Larry. "You must have *all* your magic items on a magical adventure."

Eli held out his hand.

Uncle Larry gave him a slightly used can of shoe polish. The dented can was marked $1.00.

"Um, thanks," said Eli. He shoved the half-empty tin in his back pocket.

"One more thing…" Uncle Larry put a hand to the side of his mouth, like he was about to whisper a secret.

Eli and Grace leaned in close.

"Watch out for fireballs," said Uncle Larry, then he walked off. He quickly disappeared behind the shelves of old junk and antiques.

Eli's mouth went dry. "Fireballs?"

Before either of them could ask any more questions, the door creaked open.

"Did you do that?" asked Grace.

Eli shook his head.

Then the door opened *all* the way.

"Let's go," said Grace, and she walked right out the door. She wasn't scared of a dragon.

Eli wasn't about to be shown up by his little sister. He followed her into the junkyard.

When Eli and Grace had both stepped through the door…

Everything changed.

Uncle Larry's Antique Shop & Junkyard was still there, but now it appeared to be miles away.

There was a mountain.

"Where did *that* come from?" asked Eli. He looked up past the trees, to the tip-top of the mountain.

Grace said, "I don't know, but it wasn't there a second ago. I don't like this."

"Neither do I," said Eli.

The mountain looked like they could climb it, but it would take several hours. Maybe even half a day to get to the top.

"Eli?" said Grace. "I want to go back."

Eli suddenly wanted to go back too. He also remembered what Uncle Larry had said.

Once you begin...you must finish.

"Maybe if we just..." Eli took one step toward the store, then nearly fell into a giant hole.

"Watch out!" Grace reached out to grab hold of her brother's arm. She saved him from falling into the huge crater that opened up.

The moment Eli stepped back, the hole in the earth became smaller and smaller.

The surface looked normal again.

Eli stuck his foot out.

The giant hole opened up again.

"So much for going back," said Eli. Then he turned around to face the mountain.

Trees.

Rocks.

Steep cliffs.

"Let's finish this adventure so we can go home," said Grace. "I think it's the only way we can get back to Uncle Larry's store."

Eli and Grace took a few deep breaths, then began to hike up the mountain.

6
Magic Rope

After what felt like an hour of climbing, both Eli and Grace were tired and thirsty from hiking. Looking back, they were both surprised by how far they'd come up the rocky mountainside.

"Can we rest?" asked Grace.

"Good idea," said Eli. He sat down next to his sister, then put his hubcap down beside him.

With the rays of sunshine peeking through the trees, the old hubcap looked a little bit like a shield. The kind of shield that gladiators and knights used back in ancient times.

Eli picked it up to look it over. There was nothing magical about a rusty old hubcap. If he got rid of it, that would be less for him to carry up the mountain.

"Don't throw it away, Eli," said Grace, watching her brother. "I know that's what you were thinking."

Eli smiled. Even though she could be annoying sometimes, he was glad they were together. This adventure would seem even more difficult if he were alone right now.

"Well, I guess this old hubcap is better than your useless rope," said Eli. And before she could do anything, he picked it up from where she laid it down, then tossed it over his shoulder.

"Hey!" shouted Grace. "We might need that!"

Eli noticed how big his sister's eyes were. She was staring at something behind them.

"Did you do that?" asked Grace, as her brother turned around to see.

The rope did not land on the ground.

Instead, the rope flew through the air and fastened itself to the trees. The rope went all the way up the mountain, reaching far out of sight.

It was a rope-tow, like on a skiing hill.

"I...don't think so? Maybe," said Eli. He stood up and walked over to the tree where the rope had attached itself. His hand reached out to grab it, then something strange happened.

"Whoa! Help!" shouted Eli, suddenly being pulled up the mountain. Within seconds, he was forty...sixty...eighty...one hundred feet away. He was being pulled up the hill by a magic rope.

"Wait for me!" shouted Grace, as she got to her feet. She would have to catch up quickly or else be lost on the mountain, all alone.

"Oh, no!" Grace nearly forgot to bring the items that Uncle Larry gave them. She was glad she remembered in time, and ran back to get them.

With the Scrabble game and the hubcap under one arm, she grabbed hold of the rope.

Whoosh!

Grace was off too! Her feet barely touched the ground as she glided along.

"This is fun!" shouted Grace, as she was pulled up the mountain. She got the hang of it right away, while her brother struggled to hold on.

"How do you do this?!" shouted Eli.

Slam!

"What am I supposed to do?!"

Slam!

Eli hit the ground, again and again. His face and clothes were a dirty mess. Dad would wonder what in the world happened to him.

"Look out!" came a voice behind him.

Eli turned to see Grace cruising up the mountain, coming up fast behind him.

"It's easy!" shouted Grace, as she sailed right past him. She was having a great time.

"No, it's not!" Eli shouted to her.

"It's like an escalator!" she hollered. "Just let the rope do all the work. But make sure that you keep moving your feet. Otherwise, you'll fall!"

Eli tried again.

"It works!" said Eli. His feet were going so fast, they became blurry. His shoes barely touched the ground! He was about to call to his sister, but she was too far up the mountain. Soon, only the top of her head was visible.

"Grace!" shouted Eli. "Wait for me!"

All he could do was hold onto the rope. If he didn't concentrate, he would fall over. The magic rope was pulling him along faster than the fastest mountain climber.

Grace had made it to the top, and was already going down the other side.

As Eli began to near the top, his heart started to race.

How was he going to stop?

"Oh, no!" Eli let go of the rope just as he reached the top. His momentum carried him up and over the ridge...

Then down he went, tumbling.

Eli fell down the other side of the mountain, completely out of control. He wasn't there to see his younger sister's perfect dismount. And he was thankful that she didn't see him covered in pine needles and leaves, with an acorn down his shirt.

But his terrible landing was about the last thing on his mind after he heard the crash.

And another crash.

And another.

Before each crash was a strange sound, like the noise made when you light a match.

Kk-phooof!

Only louder.

Eli said, "Sounds like...fireballs."

Grace screamed, and he ran to her.

7
Magic Shield

After each impact, the fireball would explode with a great burst of lava and smoke.

Another fireball.

Another scream.

"Grace!" shouted Eli. "Hold on, I'm coming!"

Eli didn't have time to form a plan. His brain told him to run and protect his sister, so that's what he did. He raced downhill, then slid into place beside her.

Grace was hiding behind some kind of shield. Even though she was little and the shield was huge, she was still able to hold it in place.

"What took you so long?" Grace demanded.

She looked worried and upset. "I've already been hit with twenty-six–"

CRASH!

"Twenty-*seven* fireballs," said Grace, still keeping count. "It took you that long to climb the mountain? Even with the magic rope?"

"I'm sorry," said Eli, squeezing in close beside her. There was just enough room for two kids to hide behind the large, silver shield.

"What is this thing?" asked Eli, wondering about their fireball protection. "Where did you get it? Was it just sitting here when you reached the top?"

"It's your hubcap," said Grace. "The one you were going to throw away."

The hubcap was at least ten feet high! It was so big that the biggest gladiator or even the strongest knight couldn't hold it. And it was the only thing protecting them from the fiery rocks that were raining down on them.

CRASH!

"As soon as I got to the top–" Grace stopped

to glare at her brother. "Way faster than you..."

"Yeah, yeah," said Eli.

"Well, that's when I was attacked," Grace went on. "Attacked by that...*thing* up there!"

CRASH!

"When the next fireball came shooting at me," explained Grace, "all I could think of was to hold up your old hubcap. Then it turned into a huge shield!"

CRASH!

Another fireball.

CRASH!

"And I've been here ever since," said Grace. "Waiting for you. And dodging fireballs."

CRASH!

Grace lost count of how many fireballs they'd been blasted with.

"This could go on forever," she complained.

"What's up there?" asked Eli. "How big is it? It must be huge!"

In between fireballs, both of them could hear what sounded like wings flapping. Giant wings, powerful enough to send down big gusts of wind.

Eli wanted to protect his sister, but he wasn't sure how. All they had was the magic shield, plus the old Scrabble game lying in the dirt beside them. He thought that since the rope and shield were filled with magic, then maybe the board game was another special item from Uncle Larry.

Maybe it would turn into a sword? Or a bazooka? Or a tank? Or a rocket ship, so they could blast away.

CRASH!

Eli picked up the board game. He shook it, then opened it to peek inside.

"There's the playing board, the letters, and the bag for the letters..." Eli pushed all the stuff around. "And four of those wooden things..."

CRASH!

"What are you doing now?" said Grace. "This shield won't last forever. It's starting to get hot."

"Shh!" said Eli. "I'm trying to figure this thing out. How do I get the magic to work?"

CRASH!

Eli soon gave up on the board game. He tossed the Scrabble game onto the dirt. The box popped open, and some of the letters spilled out.

"Hey!" shouted Grace. "We might need that."

Eli shook his head. "It's just a useless board game," he said. "I'm going to take a look. I need to see what's up there, so I can deal with it."

"Go ahead. Take a look," said Grace. "But you won't like it."

Eli had to see what was attacking them. Then he could come up with a plan.

After a bit of silence, with no fireball explosions, he took a peek around the side of the shield.

His sister was right. He didn't like what he saw. It was even bigger than he expected.

CRASH!

Eli ducked back behind the shield right as another fireball exploded.

"Told you," said Grace.

"That's a...it's a..." Eli was hardly able to speak.

"It's a dragon," said Grace. "The same dragon Uncle Larry told us about. It's a Word Dragon."

CRASH!

CRASH!

CRASH!

"Look!" said Eli. "Our shield!"

Up at the very top, the shield was beginning to melt away. It had protected them this long, but the magic was fading.

"This is all your fault," said Grace.

"My fault?" shouted Eli. "We went through that junkyard door together. Both of us. Remember?"

Grace had a stern look on her dirty face. "You're my big brother, so I listen to you. But not anymore. You always get me in trouble."

"Me?!"

"Yes, you."

CRASH!

The shield was turning back into a hubcap. When that happened, it would be all over.

8
Scrabble

"I've got it!" said Grace, and snapped her finger. "That has to be it! It's got to be that! It's that or nothing!"

"What?" asked Eli. "What's it? What's what?" Frustrated, he shouted, "What are you talking about?"

Without giving her brother a proper answer, Grace quickly stuffed all the letters and wooden letter blocks back into the cardboard box. Then she ran out to face the Word Dragon.

"Grace, no!" shouted Eli, but it was no use.

Grace would be no match for the dragon flying above their heads, blasting giant fireballs that could melt solid steel or even burn right through a magic hubcap.

With his back pressed up against the magic shield, Eli began to worry when the fireballs suddenly stopped.

Everything got really quiet. The whole mountain became still, which made him even more worried.

"Grace?" said Eli. "Grace, answer me!" He peeked over the top of what was left of the shield. And what he saw, he could hardly believe.

"What are you doing?!" shouted Eli.

Grace was holding up the board game like a shield—a cardboard shield, with the box all taped up, and a missing letter 'N'.

"I know what I'm doing!" hollered Grace. "Just wait, you'll see!"

"Yeah, I'll see you get blasted by a fireball any second!" shouted Eli. "What will I tell Dad?"

"Just wait, I think it's working!" said Grace. "Look, he's thinking about it! I think he wants to play!"

Eli waited for the next fireball, the one that would have her diving for cover.

But it never came.

The great big flapping dragon wings, now *those* he could still hear. But no more fireballs.

Swoop...swoop...swoop...

THUMP.

Something very big just landed.

9
The Word Dragon

Eli heard little crunching sounds, like someone small walking along a trail with dry leaves, twigs and branches.

After that, he heard loud crunching sounds, like something very big walking along a trail with dry leaves, twigs and branches.

"Will you hurry up?!" shouted Grace. "We're going to start the game without you!"

She was okay!

Eli was happy to hear her voice, but he stayed where he was. The magic shield was shrinking. He wanted to stay hidden behind it for as long as he could. Otherwise, he'd be dragon food.

When Eli dared to look, he saw his little sister playing a board game like their family did most nights after dinner. The only difference was the giant **Word Dragon** sitting beside her.

The Word Dragon had plunked its giant rear end right down on the ground. With one powerful set of claws, it very carefully selected its letters from the drawstring bag.

"We're waiting!" said Grace in her impatient voice. "Don't be scared!"

There was no use hiding behind the magic shield anymore. Their tall, super strong, fireball-stopping shield had used up all its magic. It had changed back into a regular old junky hubcap.

Eli sighed, then stood up.

What he saw was the strangest sight he'd ever seen.

Grace was seated on one of the Word Dragon's toes. Just one of its large, scaly toes was as thick as one of the trees that had fallen over during the fireball storm. She was busy choosing her letters from the bag.

"Get away from that thing!" shouted Eli. "Don't just sit there—*run*! It's going to eat you! Or blast a fireball at you!"

"Oh, stop yelling," said Grace, with her back to him. "Get over here, will you? Hurry up and pick your letters. I got some good ones!"

With a fearful heart, Eli made his way down the slope to join them. His hands were shaking, and so were his legs as he walked down the mountain.

Crunch. Crunch. Crunch.

Since the giant creature hadn't harmed his sister, he guessed—or *hoped*—that it wouldn't harm him. Or eat him. Or stomp on him. Or breathe fire on him.

Eli tried to remember what else dragons had done in all the books he'd read. None of it was good. But this dragon seemed unlike all the other dragons he'd read about. After all, he'd never heard of a Word Dragon before.

What do Word Dragons like?

They like to play Scrabble.

10
Fireball

"Finally," said Grace, as Eli joined them. "We've been waiting forever." Then she pointed to the dragon's foot, opposite where she was sitting.

Eli carefully sat down, but he kept a cautious eye on the dragon. He was ready to grab his sister and run if the creature so much as sneezed or made the slightest move to attack.

The Word Dragon looked at Eli, then nodded. The giant creature raised one powerful, scaly arm to wave at him, just like a human would do. The only difference was that the dragon had big sharp claws, each as long as the wooden letter holders from the Scrabble game.

"Choose your letters," said Grace, and tossed Eli the bag. "I've already got my word. And Mr. Word Dragon said that because it was my idea to play, I could go first."

"Please, call me Fireball," said the Word Dragon. Its voice was much deeper than anything they'd ever heard, but not a scary voice. The talking creature was extremely polite, and spoke very well for a dragon.

"Okay, Fireball." Grace seemed perfectly at ease playing Scrabble with a dragon.

Fireball the Word Dragon winked at her. The creature's eyes were bright purple, and they seemed to shine like gold.

"I am always happy to play Scrabble, my favorite game," said Fireball, "especially with such wonderful friends."

Eli was still in shock.

"See? He's a nice dragon," Grace told her brother. "And I'll bet he knows lots of words. He might win the game."

Fireball smiled, revealing great big teeth that

were longer than a seven-letter word.

"I can already tell that you two will be terrific opponents," said Fireball. "I certainly hope to keep up. Though I must warn you, I've been playing Scrabble for an awfully long time. And, just recently, I acquired a slightly used Scrabble dictionary from Uncle Larry's store."

Fireball winked again.

Grace giggled.

Eli saw no other choice but to play along. He reached a hand into the bag and drew some letters. He'd nearly forgotten how to play.

"How many letters do I draw?" asked Eli. "Seven, right?"

"Correct, Eli," said the Word Dragon.

Eli flinched.

Grace leaned over to say, "I already told him your name. Are you ready to play?"

"Yeah, I'm ready," said Eli. "I've got all my letters. Not very good ones, though. I don't think I can spell anything with this mess."

"Are you ready?" Grace asked the dragon.

"Ready when you are, Grace," said Fireball. "I will keep track of our scores." Then he reached behind his great big body and produced an old notepad. He also brought out a new pen. It was a cheap ink pen, inscribed with the words:

Uncle Larry's Antique Shop & Junkyard

CHAPTER 11
Word Games

Eli and Grace had played Scrabble lots of times with Dad. Sometimes they played their own version called "Silly Scrabble."

Silly Scrabble was where you could make up your own words. If you had a normal word, that was fine. But if your letters weren't good, you could choose to spell your own made-up word.

The tricky part of Silly Scrabble was that if you used a non-word, an illegal word like **TBOOGN**, then you had to come up with a definition for it. (Eli's definition for "tboogn" was: *picking your nose while sliding down a snowy hill on a toboggan.*)

The Word Dragon did not play Silly Scrabble. Fireball only played by the official rules.

"Look at this!" said Grace. "I can spell my name with my letters. G-R-A-C-E."

"Well done, Grace," said Fireball. "An excellent word to start off the game."

"Unless you have a better word?" Grace looked at Fireball, to see if maybe he could start the game with an even bigger word.

"Please, go ahead," said Fireball, very politely. "You may go first. Then Eli, and then me."

The Scrabble game was under way.

"G-R-A-C-E," said Grace, and put down her letters. She took extra care to make sure they were in a perfect line on the board.

"Wonderful!" said Fireball. "To do something with *grace*, means to do it with great form, elegance, and style."

"How many points is that worth?" asked Grace.

"Eight points," said Fireball, about to write her score down on the notepad.

"Don't I get double points?" asked Grace. "For

having the first word of the game?"

"Yes, you do," said Fireball. "And what's more, if you move your word slightly to the left, then the letter 'G' will land on the double letter score. You'll get even more points!"

"No thanks, right there is fine," Grace told him. "I'll leave my word right there in the middle."

The Word Dragon was impressed. "Well done, Grace. A truly noble Scrabble player, choosing to grow the board and help the other players, rather than score a few extra points."

Grace turned to her brother. "Your turn."

"Yeah, I know." Eli was having trouble with his letters. He always did okay at Scrabble, when their family played it at home. But even a good Scrabble player might have trouble with his seven letters:

L-A-A-E-E-I-O

"Do you need help?" Grace asked her brother. He looked puzzled as he shifted his letters around.

"No, I've got a word," said Eli. He connected

the first letter of his name, 'E', to the last letter of his sister's name, which was also 'E'.

E-L-I

"See? My name works too," said Eli.

When he placed his letters on the board, the Word Dragon had something to say about it.

"Ah, but your name is a proper noun," said Fireball. "So that would be an illegal word."

Eli's shoulders slumped. "Oh."

"However—" Fireball held up one long, scaly finger with a sharp claw on it. Then he leaned over the board to rearrange Eli's letters.

"If you simply move them..." said Fireball, as he shifted the letters 'I' and 'E' around, switching their places. "You can spell..."

"Lie?" said Eli. "Sure. I'll take it."

"Three points," said Fireball, then wrote it down on his notepad.

"I just hope I get some decent letters," said Eli. "I'll probably get the same letters I just put down."

"Best of luck!" said Fireball, when he carefully

handed Eli the bag of letters.

Eli groaned when he pulled another 'E' and another 'O' from the bag.

"Great. More vowels," said Eli. "Now I can spell eeeee-ahh-oo."

Grace laughed. Being silly and funny was one of her brother's best talents.

"Don't give away all your secrets, Eli," said Fireball, as he moved around his letters. "You'll never win the game if you let us know which letters you have. When playing Scrabble...or in any situation with a challenge...you should always have a strategy."

Eli sat there quietly, thinking. Not about letters or words, but about how to get away. He tried to get his sister's attention, but she was too busy thinking up her next word.

"Let's see...." said the Word Dragon, lost in his thoughts. "I could spell..."

More letter shuffling.

"Ooh! I could also spell..."

More letter shuffling.

"A-ha! I've got the perfect word. You aren't going to like this..." The Word Dragon added the letters F-U-L-L-Y to the end of Grace's word, spelling:

G-R-A-C-E-F-U-L-L-Y

"Nice one," said Grace. "And you landed on the triple word score! Wow, you really are a terrific Word Dragon."

Fireball looked very pleased with himself as he tallied up his score. "Sixty points!"

And so it went.

Two kids playing a game of Scrabble, on a mountaintop, with a dragon.

The only problem was...

How would they get back?

12
Game Plan

After twenty minutes of Scrabble, Eli and Grace began to feel quite comfortable with their situation. They were high on top of a mountain, playing Scrabble with a dragon that was completely stomping them.

So far, the scores were:

Fireball	**178 points**
Grace	**92 points**
Eli	**40 points**

Fireball came up with some good five-letter words, such as E-I-G-H-T and N-A-I-V-E, which he explained meant...'simple, or plain, or to have a lack of experience'. He also came up with some six-letter words, such as P-U-D-D-L-E and S-E-C-R-E-T. Always in great spots on the board too.

Grace came up with some good four-letter words, such as S-T-A-R and C-A-K-E. She also played some five-letter words, such as H-E-A-V-Y and C-O-U-N-T. She was extra proud of herself when she added the letters P-I-L-L-A-R to the Word Dragon's word, C-A-T-E-R.

"Caterpillar!" said Fireball. "Good show, Grace! You've changed the meaning of the word 'cater', to serve food, to that of a tiny creature that will grow up to become a beautiful butterfly."

"Thanks, Fireball," said Grace.

"Better still," continued Fireball, "your word will once again grow the board, allowing others a better chance. And perhaps help *someone* with improving their score..."

Fireball smiled at Eli, who still hadn't come up with a word that used more than three letters.

"Very funny, Fireball," said Eli.

The Word Dragon was actually very pleasant, even charming. He was a great host, when he wasn't shooting giant fireballs at them.

On his next turn, Fireball scooped up all his letters and placed them on the board.

"Seriously?" said Grace. "Not again! Do you really have another seven-letter word?"

"I'm afraid so," said Fireball with a great big grin. "Told you, I've been playing Scrabble an awfully long time."

The Word Dragon set down his seven-letter word, gaining an extra fifty points for using all his letters. He used the letter 'L' from the word caterpillar to complete his word.

"There we are," said Fireball. "Now my name is spelled out on the board too. You don't see that very often."

F-I-R-E-B-A-L-L

"Wow, you really are a Word Dragon," said Grace, amazed by the dragon's word skills.

Fireball hiccuped. "Pardon me."

Eli noticed the little trails of smoke coming out from each side of the dragon's mouth.

Grace put down the letters B-L-A-S-T for her turn. She got a triple letter score on not just one, but two different letters.

"Blast," said Grace. "Fifteen points, please."

Fireball wrote it down on the score sheet.

"Eli, it's your turn," said Grace, when she noticed her brother looking off somewhere.

"Hm? Oh. Right," said Eli, who was not having much luck so far. He only came up with smaller words, like A-T, and T-H-E, and E-A-T. During his turns, he usually just added a couple of letters to someone else's word.

This turn, Eli thought very hard. He took his time and looked all over for a good spot.

"Need help?" asked Grace.

"Nope, I got it," said Eli.

After all his staring at the board, Eli still ended up getting rid of only one letter, 'H', which he'd been trying to get rid of forever. He added the letter 'H' to the word E-A-T.

"Heat. Seven points for me," said Eli, happy because it was his best word yet.

"Not bad," said Fireball. "That's your best turn so far."

"Thanks, Fireball," said Eli, smiling. But then he let out a great big sigh when he picked out the letter 'Q' from the bag. The letter 'Q' was worth ten points just on its own, but it was one of the toughest letters to play in a game of Scrabble.

"Now, let's see..." said Fireball, shuffling around the tiny letters with his huge claws.

While they waited for the dragon to come up with a word, Eli took the opportunity to bring up something else.

"So..." said Eli, but then stopped. He had no idea how to bring up the subject.

"So...what?" said Grace. "Did you forget what you were going to say again?"

"Yeah, I guess," said Eli.

"Boys," said Grace. "So weird sometimes."

"Now, Grace," said Fireball gently, "let us all use our kind words and a soft tone of voice. As my mother used to say...*seek another's attention with kindness, not with an earth-scorching fireball.*"

That was exactly what was on Eli's mind.

Earth-scorching fireballs.

Eli didn't forget what he was going to say. He just had a tough question that he wanted to ask the dragon. Playing Scrabble was nice and all, but twenty minutes ago, Fireball the dragon was blasting lava rocks down at them.

Why had he done it?

"Don't be shy, Eli," said Fireball. "We are having a nice, civilized game of Scrabble. All conversation topics are welcome here. If you have a question, please ask. I will do my best to answer."

"Well, okay," said Eli, still sounding unsure. "I was just wondering..."

"Yes?" said Fireball. He was thinking hard while he shuffled his letters around. Thinking and shuffling, and tapping one huge claw on his long, pointy chin, with all the sharp teeth poking out.

"I was just wondering," said Eli. "Um, why..."

"Say it!" said Grace. "Just ask him, will you? You're driving me crazy."

"Okay, okay," said Eli.

Fireball finally put his word down. It was a five-letter word, B-E-A-S-T. But combined with the connecting word, it was still worth twenty-seven points.

Eli cleared his throat. He was worried this might be the last question he would ever ask. A simple question, which he *hoped* would not lead to another fireball attack.

13
Escape

"Why were you shooting fireballs at us?" Eli finally asked. "Did we do something wrong? Are you angry at us?"

Fireball sniffed.

"I do apologize for that," said Fireball. "Though, it is my nature to do so, being a dragon. Honestly, I was just happy to have visitors."

"That's okay, Fireball," said Grace. "Can all dragons do that? Shoot big fireballs like you can?"

Fireball had to think. "Some of us breathe fire, while other dragons use their powerful tail. And some dragons, like me, are able to produce boulders soaked with fire, then spit them out.

Kind of like how you humans *sneeze*."

Grace laughed. "You're funny."

Fireball laughed too.

Eli would have laughed, but what they were talking about was dangerous. Shooting a fiery rock that was big enough to put a huge crater in the ground or snap an evergreen tree in half was definitely no kids' game.

Scrabble was less dangerous.

While the Word Dragon was choosing his letters from the bag, Grace asked another question. She wanted to know what came next, when the game was over.

"Hey, Fireball?"

"Yes, Grace?" said Fireball.

"What happens when the Scrabble game is over?" she asked. "When all the letters are gone and there are no more words to play?"

Fireball hiccuped. "Well, I suppose we will have to go back..." Another hiccup. "Sorry. I've been eating too many rocks lately."

"That's okay," said Grace, then she giggled.

Eli did not laugh. He had read enough about dragons to know that some of them, like Fireball, ate rocks, then digested them with the lava in their super strong stomach. And that's how they were able to shoot fireballs.

"Well, Grace, to answer your question," said Fireball, "I suppose we will have to go back to what we were doing before the game."

Eli's eyes were huge. "Before?"

What they were doing *before* the Scrabble game was getting blasted with fireballs. Before the game, they had giant burning rocks raining down on them from the sky.

"Oh, dear! You are not going to like this," said Fireball, then his large purple eyes lit up.

"What is it?" asked Grace.

"It appears..." Fireball shuffled his letters once more. "Yes, it appears that I may have another seven-letter word lined up."

Grace looked at her brother, then winked.

Eli had no idea what his little sister was up to, but he didn't want the dragon to get suspicious.

Fireball was too busy with his words to notice.

"Hey, Fireball?"

"Yes, Grace?"

"My brother and I, we have to, um..." Grace looked over her shoulder. "We have to go over there...to that tree. Just for a second, okay?"

Eli tried not to freak out. He thought for sure they'd get caught. This was the worst L-I-E he had ever heard. It was not done G-R-A-C-E-F-U-L-L-Y at all. It made the moment very A-W-K-W-A-R-D, which was one of Fireball's seven-letter words.

There was no way the Word Dragon was going to fall for it. And even if he did fall for it, then what? If he got mad or suspected something, how were they going to outrun a dragon? Especially one that could shoot giant fireballs out of its mouth?

"Fine, fine, go ahead," said Fireball. "I've got what I believe is another excellent word here, but I want to double-check the spelling. My Scrabble dictionary is in my cave."

Whoosh!

The Word Dragon took flight from right where

it was sitting. Its great powerful wings kicked up so much wind that both Eli and Grace were knocked to the ground.

The game was left untouched. Not a single letter or word was disturbed in the least, as if the Word Dragon had sprinkled some kind of magic Scrabble dust onto the board game, so none of the letters would move.

"Be back in a few minutes!" hollered Fireball, from up in the sky.

As soon as the dragon was out of sight, Eli and Grace ran for cover under the trees.

Neither of them moved. They just stood there, looking nervously up at the sky.

"Okay, so what's the next part of your plan?" asked Eli. He was ready to move. Ready to leave.

"What do you mean *next* part?" said Grace. "My plan was to get us away from the Scrabble game so *you* could think up a way for us to escape. "

"What?!" shouted Eli. "I don't have an escape plan! I thought you did!"

Grace crossed her arms. "You are my big

brother," she said, "so *you* are supposed to think of stuff like how to escape from a dragon."

Eli was ready to pop. "Fine," he said. Then he stood there on top of the mountain, trying to come up with a plan.

Any plan, any idea.

The sky was silent and clear. But not for much longer. The dragon's cave was nearby, which meant Fireball would be back any minute.

"Well?" Grace tapped her foot in the dirt.

"I'm thinking!" said Eli.

"Well, you better think faster," said Grace. "We don't have much time. Soon we'll be in big trouble. The worst kind of trouble. Dragon trouble."

Whoosh-whoosh-whoosh...

Fireball was already coming back.

"I've got the dictionary!" shouted Fireball, somewhere above their heads. They couldn't see him through the tall trees and thick forest.

"It is just as I thought," said Fireball. "My word is correct! A perfectly legal Scrabble word!"

"That's great, Fireball!" said Grace, shouting

into the sky. Her voice rose above the trees.

"R-U-I-N-A-T-E!" shouted Fireball. "It means, of course, to bring something to ruin!"

Eli was being pushed. His little sister was shoving him, urging him to say something.

"That's, um...great, Fireball!" Eli hollered up to the dragon. "But we're going to leave now, okay? It was nice to meet you! Bye!"

Eli and Grace raced back up to the top of the mountain, then started to climb down the other side, back to the magic rope.

"Thanks for the game, Fireball!" shouted Grace. "Maybe we can play Scrabble again someday! Bye!"

There was silence on top of the mountain. Only the steady flapping of dragon wings, somewhere above their heads.

And then came the fireballs.

CRASH!

Another storm of fiery rocks rained down. All around them, trees were exploding in a shower of sparks, then catching on fire.

The Word Dragon realized that he had been tricked. Fireball wasn't mad. He was mostly disappointed that his two new friends, Eli and Grace, were running away. And he was a little sad that they wouldn't be able to finish the game. This would make it an I-N-C-O-M-P-L-E-T-E game of Scrabble.

CRASH!

Another fireball.

"Do you think he's mad?" said Grace.

"Yes, he's shooting fireballs at us!" said Eli, as he ducked for cover behind an evergreen tree.

"Maybe he just has an upset stomach," said Grace. She screamed when a fireball struck the tree beside her, sending sparks everywhere. The tree was at least sixty feet high, but the burning fireball split it right in half.

"Grace!" shouted Eli. He reached out his hand just in time, and pulled his sister to safety, right before the tree came crashing down.

"You okay?" asked Eli, panting.

"Yes, I'm okay," said Grace. "Barely."

CRASH!

"What do we do now?" asked Grace. Her eyes were filling with tears because she was scared, and also because of the smoke.

"RUN!" shouted Eli.

And that's exactly what they did. They ran back down the mountainside, as fast as they could, while great fireballs rained down from the sky.

14
Danger

Eli and Grace made it down to the magic rope, which was still attached to the trees. And, thankfully, the magic still worked.

"Grab hold of the rope!" said Eli. "Let's get away from that Scrabble Dragon!"

"He's a Word Dragon," Grace corrected him.

"He's a fireball-shooting dragon!" shouted Eli. "Just go!"

The moment her hand touched the magic rope, Grace went speeding down the mountain.

Eli grabbed hold too, and they both went down the mountain slope so fast that their feet were hardly able to keep up with the quick pace.

Fireball the Word Dragon moved fast.

So did the fireballs.

CRASH!

Grace turned around to look at her brother, then nearly tripped. Luckily, she stayed on her feet as the magic rope pulled her down the mountain.

"Don't let go of the rope!" said Eli, but with all the explosions, he had no idea if she could hear him. "Don't stop, just keep going!"

CRASH!

Trees exploded on the left, on the right, in front and behind. Everywhere they looked, smoke filled the air, and red-hot sparks came down like glowing rain.

CRASH!

As they continued to race down the mountain, Eli and Grace both realized they had a huge problem waiting for them at the bottom.

What if the ground opened up again?

What if the earth tried to swallow them?

Last time, a giant hole opened up when Eli stuck out his foot and tried to go back. That great big hole in the earth had been wide enough to swallow him and his sister.

CRASH!

More fallen trees.

More explosions.

CRASH!

Fireball didn't want to scare off his new friends. Instead, he wanted them to come back and play another game of Scrabble.

CRASH!

Eli had to dream up the next part of their escape plan. He remembered what Uncle Larry had told them: *'If you choose to take on this adventure, you have to complete it—otherwise you shouldn't even start. Once you begin...you must finish.'*

Eli got to thinking.

Technically, they didn't finish the Scrabble game. When they ran off, there were still a few letters left in the bag. He nearly had the word D-R-A-G-O-N, but was missing one letter 'N'.

15
Challenge

Once Eli and Grace reached the bottom of the mountain, they knew they were in serious trouble.

Above their heads was bright blue sky. But spread out before them was nothing but flat, dry land, without a single tree in sight.

Nowhere to hide from the dragon.

Straight ahead of them was Uncle Larry's Antique Shop & Junkyard. But it was miles away.

There was no sign of Dad or Uncle Larry, so they were on their own.

"We'll never make it," said Eli. "That Word Dragon will get us long before we make it to Uncle Larry's store."

"I miss Dad," said Grace.

Eli felt bad because he was the older brother, which meant he was supposed to protect his younger sister. But he was scared too. They needed a grownup, but there were none around. It was just them against a fireball-shooting dragon that was really good at Scrabble.

"Oh no," said Grace. "Look."

Fireball was right above them. Each time the creature flapped his powerful wings, it sent down a huge gust of hot air.

"I do apologize for this!" shouted Fireball.

CRASH!

Down came another fireball.

Both Eli and Grace had to dive out of the way.

"You were both wonderful playmates!" shouted Fireball. "I do hope you will join me for another game of Scrabble!"

CRASH!

CRASH!

"That's okay, Fireball!" Grace shouted up to him. "It's not your fault! You're a dragon!"

"Don't apologize to him!" said Eli, getting mad. "He's trying to blast us out of the universe!"

"No, he's not," said Grace. "He's just got a sore stomach, is all."

Eli and Grace ran as fast as they could.

Uncle Larry's Antique Shop was still a long way off. There was no way they would be able to outrun Fireball and his fireball attack.

Unless...

There was one more magic item.

"Wait! I have an idea!" shouted Eli, and he and his sister both stopped running.

Eli looked up and shouted, "Hey, Fireball?"

"Yes, Eli?"

CRASH!

They both had to jump out of the way when another flaming rock hit the ground. It left a huge crater in the dry, cracked earth.

"Since you were going to win the last Scrabble game anyway..."

CRASH!

Eli jumped.

"...maybe we should start..."

CRASH!

"...a new game?"

CRASH!

"What do you say?"

Fireball was only a dark shadow up in the sky. He continued to flap his mighty wings.

No fireballs, though.

The ancient creature looked down at the two small figures on the ground. He thought very hard about the offer, since a Word Dragon never turns down a game of Scrabble.

The silence was making Eli nervous. He wasn't sure if his plan was working or if he and his sister were two seconds from another fireball attack.

16
Magic Goop

"Challenge accepted!" said Fireball.

Grace wasn't sure what was happening or what Eli was doing. But she trusted her brother.

"Okay, great!" said Eli. "We just need to go over there, to Uncle Larry's store! We need to ask our dad if we're allowed to play Scrabble with a dragon. We'll be right–"

CRASH!

"–back."

The fireball burned and crackled beside them.

"Not so fast, Eli," said Fireball. "We should begin the game now. Forget about going back. Forget about everything."

"Everything?" asked Grace. "Even Dad?"

"You both belong to me now," said Fireball. "We can play Scrabble from now until the end of time. That sounds like a wonderful plan to me."

Grace looked worried. "The end of time?" she said. "But I don't know that many words."

Eli was ready to test out his plan.

Not a *good* plan, but it was something to try. If it failed, they would be trapped here, forced to play Scrabble with a Word Dragon forever.

"Hey, look at that!" said Eli. "My shoelace is untied. I better fix it..."

Eli bent down to tie his shoe. But he wasn't really tying his shoelace. He pulled the half-empty tin of shoe polish out of his jeans pocket. He rubbed some on his shoes, then whispered to Grace.

"*Pssst!* Get—over—here!" Eli waved at her to come closer, and to crouch down next to him.

"I am not tying your shoelace," said Grace. "You're the one who taught *me*, remember?"

"Just give me your feet," said Eli. "Hurry up, we

don't have much time." He jabbed his finger into the squishy shoe polish, then quickly rubbed it all over Grace's shoes.

"My shoes!" said Grace. "Dad is going to be so mad at you for putting that yucky goop all over my brand-new shoes."

"*Shhh*, be quiet," said Eli. "It's magic goop."

"Oh." Grace was no longer angry.

Fireball was still right above their heads, flapping his wings. He was ready for them all to head back up the mountain.

"All done?" asked Fireball.

"Yes, all done!" hollered Eli.

"Good! Now we should all go back up to the top," said Fireball. "After another game of Scrabble, we will find you a cozy cave to sleep in. You can take a bath in the nice cold river, then you can catch mice for supper. All you can eat!"

"Eww, gross!" Grace said quietly. "I am *not* eating mice. You don't eat mice, you play with them."

"I'm not eating mice, either," said Eli. "*Ugh*."

Even though they had just run down an entire mountain, neither Eli or Grace were out of breath, thanks to the magic rope. And now they were about to sprint all the way to Uncle Larry's store, using some more magic.

They hoped.

Eli had one final part of his plan. Now, a clever person would never fall for such an obvious trick. But this was a Word Dragon. And if there was one thing that a Word Dragon loved more than anything, it was...

Words.

Tricky words.

Q-words.

17
Qi, Qadi, Qigong

"Do you know any good 'Q' words?" Eli shouted way up into the sky. "Words that begin with the letter 'Q'?"

Fireball was delighted.

The Word Dragon's sparkly purple eyes lit up, and his rows of sharp teeth spread into a smile. He loved any chance to talk about his two favorite subjects: words and word games.

"I'm glad you asked, Eli," said Fireball. "Now, first let me tell you a little bit about the history of the alphabet. It all started back in ancient Egypt..."

While Fireball was babbling about the history of the alphabet, Eli whispered to his sister.

"Run," said Eli.

"What?"

"Run!" he said louder. "Get to Uncle Larry's store. Don't look behind you, just run. Got it?"

"Okay," said Grace. "I will r-uuuuuun!"

Eli had to shield his face from all the sand that his sister's feet kicked up. Grace took off running so fast that she was soon out of sight.

The magic goop worked!

Once his sister was a safe distance away, Eli stood up to face the Word Dragon.

"That's all great information, Fireball," said Eli, "but what about—"

"Hold on, I'm getting there," said Fireball. Then he started talking about previous Scrabble games, ones he'd played in the past.

Eli was forced to listen to the Word Dragon talk about all the unusual words he had ever used while playing Scrabble.

M-U-U-M-U-U, a type of dress.

U-L-U, a knife.

I-N-C-O-N-N-U, a large fish.

"And don't forget P-I-N-G-U-I-D," said Fireball, "a word that means 'greasy'!"

Eli was getting hot and sweaty from standing in the sun. He was ready to bolt. But he had to wait for the right opportunity.

"Those are all great Scrabble words, Fireball," said Eli, "but I was asking about Q-words!"

"Ah, right!" said Fireball. "The letter 'Q' is perhaps the most difficult one to get rid of in a game of Scrabble!"

Eli got ready to run.

Now was his only chance to get away, since Fireball was so distracted by words.

"Here...we...go!" said Eli.

The magic shoe polish kicked in.

And he was off!

Eli was soon racing across the land at an incredible speed, just like a superhero.

"Hey, down there! Where are you going?" shouted Fireball. "Where are you running off to?"

"Sorry, Fireball!" hollered Eli. "It's not me, it's my feet! There's magic in my shoes!"

"Eli, I wasn't finished yet! I was just getting to the good part!" shouted Fireball, chasing after the speedy boy. "I have a whole list of Q-words you can use!"

The attack came quickly.

CRASH!

Fireball did an excellent job of matching the speed of Eli's magic shoes. The fireballs were getting more and more A-C-C-U-R-A-T-E.

Eli could feel the heat from the fireballs as he ran. He jumped out of the way each time.

CRASH!

While running at a terrific speed across the dry land, Eli shouted, "I know a few Q-words! There's Q-U-I-T, and Q-U-I-E-T..."

"Very good, Eli!" said Fireball. "But what happens when you have the letter 'Q' but do not have the letter 'U' available? What then?"

Eli could hardly keep up with his own feet! He ran faster than any kid at school had ever dreamed of running.

"Try the two-letter word Q-I," said Fireball.

"That word is pronounced the same as K-E-Y. It is a type of spiritual energy!"

CRASH!

"Or the four-letter word Q-A-D-I," continued Fireball, "which is a type of public official!"

Eli ran.

He ran, and ran.

The junkyard was getting closer, but he still had a long way to go. Eli had never run this far in his life—not even if he took the last fifty school races and stuck them all together.

Grace was yelling something, but Eli couldn't understand. She was too far away.

"Or the six-letter word S-H-E-Q-E-L," said Fireball, "which is a very old way to measure the weight of something, usually precious stones, such as gems and diamonds."

CRASH!

"That's all really interesting, Fireball!" shouted Eli. "Any others?"

"There is also Q-I-V-I-U-T," explained Fireball, "which is the wool of a musk-ox!"

CRASH!

"That word has a 'U' in it!" shouted Eli.

"That is true, Eli! My mistake!" said Fireball. "But how about M-B-A-Q-A-N-G-A, which is pronounced *muh-kang-uh*. It is a type of South African dance music!"

"Good one!" said Eli.

"Although..." said Fireball, "at eight letters, I have never once seen or even heard of the word mbaqanga being played in a game of Scrabble."

CRASH!

"And one of my all-time favorites is the word Q-W-E-R-T-Y," Fireball went on, "which is the word to describe how all the letters and numbers are arranged on a computer keyboard!"

Eli dodged fireballs left and right.

"Any other Q-words?" he asked.

Fireball the Word Dragon knew them all.

"There's Q-A-N-A-T, a tunnel that is located underground..."

CRASH!

"Let's not forget Q-I-G-O-N-G!" said Fireball.

"That Q-word—pronounced *chee-guhng*—means exercise or meditation! And if that word is placed well on the board—say, on a triple word score—you would earn fifty-four points!"

CRASH!

"Or you could add the letter 'S' to spell the word Q-I-G-O-N-G-S," said Fireball, "and make it plural. Worth sixty-three points!"

CRASH!

"Isn't that interesting, Eli?"

CRASH!

"You bet, Fireball!" shouted Eli, running and dodging. "I could talk about Scrabble all day!"

"So could I, Eli!" said Fireball. "So could I."

CRASH!

The junkyard was finally getting close. If Eli could keep up this pace just a little while longer, he just might make it to safety.

His heart sank to the bottom of his shoes when his running speed began to fade.

He was slowing down.

The magic was wearing off.

CHAPTER
18
The Biggest Fireball

"Come on, shoes!" Eli felt foolish for yelling at his own shoes. But the junkyard was so close, and he wasn't going to make it.

Grace was waving at him to keep going. She didn't understand why he was slowing down.

Eli was running at normal speed.

The magic shoe polish had worn off.

Maybe he hadn't used enough?

CRASH!

Whatever the cause, Eli was about to get blasted with the biggest, baddest, most humongous fireball of all time.

Fireball hiccuped. "Oh, dear..."

The Word Dragon, as he told them earlier, had eaten a lot of rocks lately. And that's why he didn't feel good. And why he had the hiccups. And it was also the reason he was blasting so many fireballs.

Fireball had an upset stomach.

"Sorry about this, Eli!" said Fireball. "Too bad we didn't get to finish our Scrabble game!"

Eli could finally hear his sister calling to him.

"Hurry up!" shouted Grace "Dad's waiting!"

Eli knew he wasn't going to make it. And he knew what was coming, but he still had to try.

Fireball's stomach gurgled. Smoke was coming out of his mouth, his nostrils, even his long scaly ears. All those rocks in his stomach had melted into one big, flaming ball of hot, molten lava. And it was about to come blasting out.

Eli wasn't really mad at Fireball for shooting lava rocks at him. He loved dragons, and books about dragons, and movies with dragons, even dragon puzzles. He even had a special place in his heart for "Petey," his stuffed dragon toy, which he had recently given to his little sister.

"Goodbye, Eli!" said Fireball.

Then out came a fireball as big as a used car from Uncle Larry's junkyard. It was huge!

At the very last second...

Eli jumped through the air.

And then...

C-R-A-S-H

Eli made it.

He and his sister rushed through the junkyard, then raced into Uncle Larry's shop.

Uncle Larry was behind the cash register. Dad had his wallet out, and was paying for their brand-new, slightly used lawnmower.

Dad looked at Eli, then at Grace. He wondered why they looked like they'd just run a marathon. Big eyes, breathing heavy, and dirty faces.

Dad asked, "What happened to you two?"

CHAPTER 19
Lawnmower

The next morning, Eli was about to mow the lawn for the first time. Dad was there to help, in case Eli ran into trouble. Pushing a real lawnmower for the first time was a big deal, but Eli was ready for the challenge.

"Ear plugs, check..." said Dad. "Safety glasses, check...work gloves, check..."

"Dad, come on! I've got this," said Eli. He was ready to go. And ready to mow!

Eli was going to be the first one to test out the lawnmower they bought from Uncle Larry's Antique Shop & Junkyard, where just yesterday Eli and Grace had a very B-I-G adventure.

"Okay, Eli," said Dad. "Go for it!"

Eli pulled the cord to the lawnmower, just like Dad showed him. It cranked right up, first try.

BRUUUUM-bruum-bruumm...

Even Dad was impressed.

"See? I told you Uncle Larry had some good stuff at his store," said Dad.

Eli looked very proud holding onto a rumbling lawnmower. He was mowing the lawn like a big kid, under the careful watch of Dad.

"Let me know when you get tired!" said Dad, who had to yell so Eli could hear him.

Eli gave him a thumbs-up.

Grace was sitting on the patio. She had a blanket spread out, with cups and plates, and napkins folded up nice and neat. She was treating her favorite new stuffed animal to a delicious brunch.

"You good?" asked Dad.

"I'm good!" Eli shouted back.

When Eli came around in a circle, he carefully mowed the grass next to the patio.

As Eli pushed the lawnmower past his sister, he hollered to her, "Are you okay?"

Grace nodded and gave her big brother a thumbs-up. She was wearing Dad's cool new ear muffs that he bought from Uncle Larry's store.

She was proud of Eli, her very brave older brother. But the noise was interrupting her tea party with her stuffed animal—a dragon.

"You're not 'Petey' anymore," said Grace. "Your new name is...Fireball."

CHAPTER 20
New Ladder

After all the chores were done, Dad and Eli joined Grace for brunch. Since she was out of pretend juice and pretend scones, she asked Dad if they could have a real snack.

"Excellent idea, Grace," said Dad. He went into the kitchen to fix them all something to eat.

Eli sat down on Grace's favorite picnic blanket, the one she'd had since she was little.

"Eww!" Grace pushed his legs. "You're getting gross stuff all over my blanket!"

"Sorry!" Eli moved back so he wouldn't get her blanket all grassy and sweaty.

Grace fixed the blanket so it was just right.

Then she handed him a paper towel to sit on.

"How did I do?" asked Eli. "Mowing the lawn, I mean. It's fun, but only for a little while. Then your arms get tired, and it stops being fun."

Grace looked at her brother, then the freshly cut lawn, and then her stuffed dragon.

"Mowing the lawn is fine," said Grace, "but I'm mostly glad you can protect me from a dragon."

Eli smiled.

"We're out of juice!" Dad called from the kitchen. "Lemonade okay?"

Eli and Grace both said, "That's fine!"

While waiting for their drinks and snack to arrive, Eli and Grace spoke in quiet voices about their wild adventure: climbing a mountain, dodging fireballs, and hanging out with the Word Dragon.

Dad came back out, and they stopped.

"Here we are," said Dad, "some fruit, some veggies, some chips, and some fresh lemonade."

Eli put a finger to his lips, so Grace wouldn't say anything about what happened. They still hadn't told Dad about their junkyard adventure, and how much fun they'd had at Uncle Larry's.

"What were you whispering about?" asked Dad, as he set the snack tray down.

"Oh, nothing important," said Eli. "We were just talking about the, um, lawnmower."

"Yeah," Grace agreed. "Just talking."

Dad sat down on the blanket with them, and poured himself a glass of lemonade. He was so hot and sweaty from helping Eli mow the lawn, he drank a whole glass of lemonade in one long gulp. Then he poured himself another glass.

During their brunch on the patio, Dad noticed a small crack in the siding of the house. They had just moved in a few weeks ago, so there were lots of things that needed work.

"Uh-oh," said Dad. "I'd better fix that."

Eli and Grace looked where he was pointing, way up high, close to the roof. Just underneath the gutter, there was a two-inch hole in one of the siding panels of the house.

"Can I help?" asked Eli.

"Me too," said Grace. "I'm a helper."

Dad laughed. "Yes, you can both help. But that's very high. We'll need a ladder."

"We can use the stepladder," said Grace. "It's still in my bedroom, from when you were helping me hang my art pictures."

"Good idea, Grace," said Dad, "but that stepladder isn't quite tall enough. We'll have to go buy a new ladder."

Eli and Grace looked at each other. They were both thinking the same thing.

"A used ladder?" suggested Grace.

"From Uncle Larry's store?" said Eli.

Dad thought about it, then nodded.

"Another good idea," said Dad. "I wonder if Uncle Larry has a ladder for sale? Come to think of it...I'm pretty sure I saw a few ladders while I was out back in the junkyard..."

Eli got excited.

Grace got excited too.

Sounded like another adventure!

Dad finished his second glass of lemonade,

and then he stood up and stretched his back.

"Maybe I'll swing by Uncle Larry's store this afternoon," said Dad, thinking out loud.

Eli and Grace both smiled.

"Can we go, too?"

Dear friends,

Here is a list of words used in the book. These are the same words that Eli, Grace, and myself used during our game.

Perhaps they will come in handy if you play a game of Scrabble with your family...or if you and I ever get the chance to play together.

Your dragon friend,
Fireball

Scrabble Words

(in order of appearance in the book)

Grace [*grays*]: to give beauty to

Lie [*lahy*]: to speak falsely

Gracefully [*grays-fuhl-ee*]: displaying grace in form or action

Eight [*eyt*]: a number (one more than seven)

Naïve [*nah-eve*]: deficient in worldly or informed judgment

Puddle [*puhd-l*]: small pool of water

Secret [*see-krit*]: something that is kept from knowledge or view

Star [*stahr*]: a natural luminous body visible in the sky

Cake [*keyk*]: a bread-like food made from dough or batter that is baked or fried

Heavy [*hev-ee*]: having much weight

Count [*kount*]: to list or mention the units of one by one to ascertain the total

Pillar [*pil-er*]: to provide with vertical building supports

Cater [*key-ter*]: to provide food

Caterpillar [*kat-uh-pil-er*]: the elongated worm-like larva of a butterfly or moth

Fireball [*fahyuh-r-bawl*]: a luminous meteor

Blast [*blahst*]: to use an explosive

At [*ah-t*]: a word used to indicate presence or occurrence in, on, or near

The [*th-uh*]: definite article

Eat [*eet*]: to consume food

Heat [*heet*]: to make hot

Beast [*beest*]: a large, four-footed mammal

Awkward [*awk-werd*]: lacking skill or dexterity

Ruinate [*roo-uh-neyt*]: to ruin

Incomplete [*in-kuhm-pleet*]: not complete

Muumuu [*moo-moo*]: a long, loose dress

Ulu [*oo-loo*]: a short knife with a broad blade

Inconnu [*in-kuh-noo*]: an unknown person or thing

Pinguid [*ping-gwid*]: oily or greasy

Accurate [*ak-yer-it*]: contains no error or defect

Quit [*kwit*]: to give up, depart from, or opt out

Quiet [*kwahy-it*]: make little or no noise

Qi [*kee*]: the vital force in Chinese thought that is inherent in all things

Key [*kee*]: a (usually) metal instrument by which the bolt of a lock is turned

Qadi [*kah-dee*]: a Muslim judge

Sheqel [*shek-uhl*]: an ancient unit of weight

Qiviut [*kee-vee-uht*]: the wool of a musk-ox

Mbaqanga: [*muh-kang-uh*]: a South African dance music

Qwerty [*kwur-tee*]: a standard keyboard

Qanat [*kahn-aht*]: a system of tunnels and wells

Qigong [*chee-goo-ng*]: a Chinese system of physical exercises

Qigongs [*chee-goo-ng-z*]: plural of qigong

About the Author

Tevin Hansen is the multi-award-winning author of more than 20 middle grade books, including *Hole in the Wall*, *Hairytale Adventures*, and the *Junkyard Adventures* series. He enjoys writing fast-paced, humorous books for kids, and also the occasional YA novel. Tevin lives in Lincoln, Nebraska, with his wife, kids, and a collection of cheap guitars.

Discover more at:
www.tevinhansen.com or follow Tevin on Facebook, Instagram, YouTube and Twitter.

Leave an Amazon review...

...get a free poster!

Help us reach our goal
of 100+ reviews per book.

Visit **www.TevinHansen.com** for more information.

JUNKYARD ADVENTURES
www.junkyardadventures.com

A JUNKYARD ADVENTURE

W O R D
Dragon

TEVIN HANSEN

Play an epic game
of Scrabble with
the Word Dragon.

A JUNKYARD ADVENTURE

GIANT
of GEOGRAPHY

TEVIN HANSEN

Sea Serpent
of SCIENCE

TEVIN HANSEN

Visit the seven
continents with the
Giant of Geography.

Discover the
ocean with the Sea
Serpent of Science.

What constellation will you find with the Alien of Astronomy?

A JUNKYARD ADVENTURE

Alien of Astronomy

TEVIN HANSEN

A JUNKYARD ADVENTURE

Mermaid of Music

Music Crafts Inside

TEVIN HANSEN

Make a beautiful melody with the Mermaid of Music.

A JUNKYARD ADVENTURE

Art Monster

CRAFT PROJECTS INSIDE

TEVIN HANSEN

Get creative with the Art Monster.

Hairytale Adventures

Read all three Alexia & Melvin chapter books!

Alexia and Melvin have a complicated relationship. And that mean old bear doesn't make things any easier.

Made in the USA
Las Vegas, NV
10 December 2022

61718031R00069